Read•A•Picture

LET'S GO

By Burton Marks
Illustrated by Paul Harvey

JOSHUA MORRIS PUBLISHING

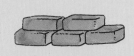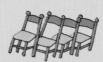

ON RAINY NIGHTS

On rainy nights when I'm tucked into  ,

dreamy thoughts go through my head.

I hear the patter of the  ,

and look! My 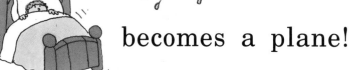 becomes a plane!

It whizzes out the ,

and soars above the .

I wave to all the passing ,

the , and .

The below looks very small;

I cannot see my at all.

The places where I always play

are tiny from far away.

I journey past the 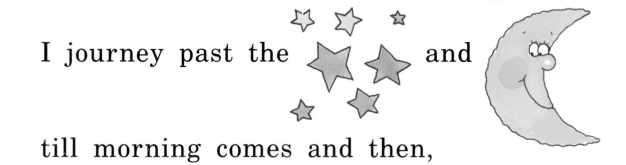 and

till morning comes and then,

my plane flies back into my room,

and becomes my  again.

FIND-A-PICTURE

Somewhere in this picture are:

a [ship], a [train], a [car], a [airplane], and a [crane truck]. Can you find them?

OFF I GO!

I'm taking a ✈ to Japan,

I'm boarding a 🚆 for Pakistan,

I'm flying a 🚀 up to the 🌙,

and I won't be back any time soon.

I'm riding my 🚲 to Peru,

I'm driving a 🚗 to Timbuktu,

I'm sailing a ⛵ to Bombay,

I must be going—if Mum says it's OK.

MY LITTLE CAR

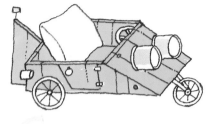

I have a shiny little

It's ever so much fun.

I never stop to fill it up—

it needs my  to make it run.

MY "JUST PRETEND" TRAIN

My  is just four kitchen

 lined up in a row.

But it can take me anywhere

that I would like to go.

I can cross the highest  ,

I can ride down to the sea,

or go deep into the

if that's what pleases me.

I can journey to a

in a land far, far away.

Because my  is "just pretend"

it takes me where I want to play.

PICTURE A RIDDLE

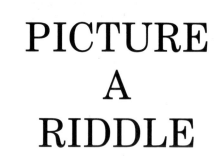

• What bird can lift heavy things?

• What has one horn, runs all day and gives milk?

• What did they call the first bus in America?

• What do you call a sleeping bull?

• Who has teeth but cannot bite?

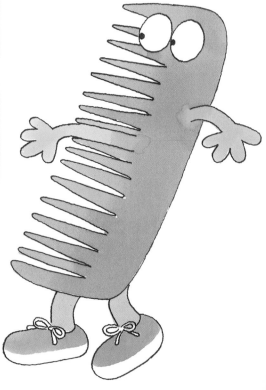

• milk float
• bulldozer
• Columbus
• crane
• comb

MY BOAT OF WOOD AND NAILS

One day I took some 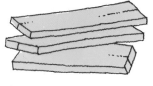 and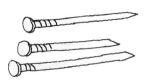

and made a little  .

I put it in the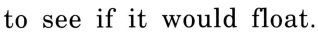

to see if it would float.

It drifted quickly out to sea,

the 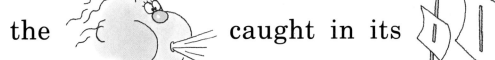 caught in its 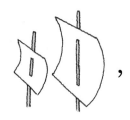 ,

and I never ever saw it again,

my  of 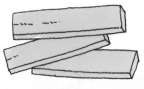 and 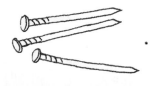 .

MY VERY OWN SPACESHIP

I'm building my own spaceship

from things I have on hand—

 , rocks, a cardboard 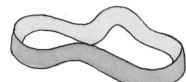 ,

a giant rubber 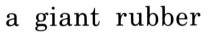 .

Roller  and paper plates,

mops and 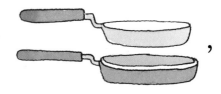 and frying 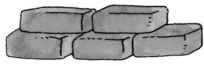,

toothpicks,  and ice cream sticks,

safety 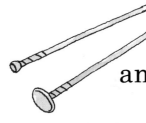 and rubbish bins,

poppers, zips and bottle ,

 and pails and worn-out ,

strings and and mattress ,

 nuts and bolts and metal .

I've been working since this morning
and I cannot figure why,
when I started up the engine
my spaceship wouldn't fly!

I've checked and rechecked everything—
I'm not sure what to do.
Do you think perhaps it needs
another bottle or **2**?

LITTLE BEAR'S BIRTHDAY

Little Bear is having a party today.

Look! All the guests are on their way.

Can you name the things
that each one brings?

Presents, presents everywhere.
Happy Birthday, Little Bear!

FIND-A-PICTURE

Somewhere in this picture are:

 a , a , a , a , and a . Can you find them?

THE LONG-LEGGED CRANE

Jane McShane is a long-legged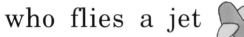

who flies a jet

when she travels to Spain. Unless, of course,

it happens to , in which case

you might see her taking a

BARNEY MULDOON

Barney Muldoon is a clever

who can play the bassoon by the light of the  .

And sometimes in June, in the late afternoon,

he may play you a tune in his hot-air

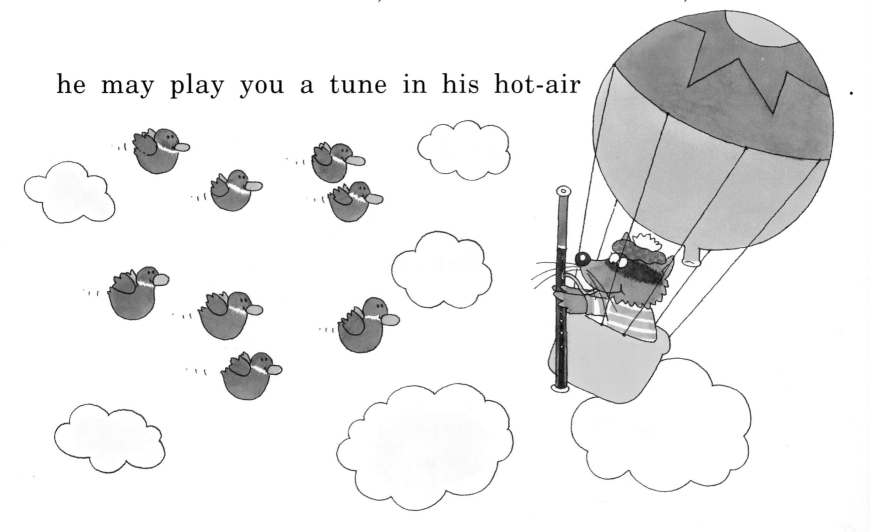

We p 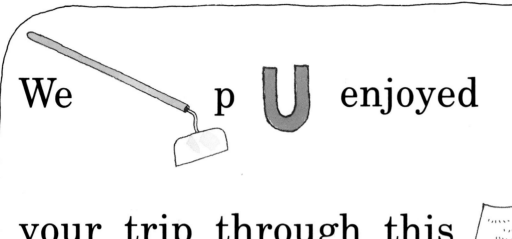 enjoyed

your trip through this  .

Please come back 4 another look!